Eighteen Cousins

By Carol G. Hogan

Illustrated by Beverly Komoda

PARENTS' MAGAZINE PRESS · NEW YORK

To Kelly, Terry, Tracy, Shaun and Molly

I went for a visit,
I went to a farm.
I went to my cousins'
When it was warm.

I went to my cousins'
(Whom I'd never seen)
I counted my cousins . . .
And I counted EIGHTEEN!

I looked at a horse
Down on the farm,

I looked at a pig
Out by the barn.

I looked at a cow
(And it was a she)

I looked at a lamb . . .

But what did I see?

EIGHTEEN COUSINS a-looking at me!

I watched baby chickens
Scratch on the ground,
I watched baby ducklings
Waddle around.

I watched a new gosling
Peck at a tree,
I watched an old rooster . . .
But what did I see?

EIGHTEEN COUSINS a-watching me!

I sniffed at the sky,
I sniffed at the air,
I sniffed at the flowers
That grew everywhere.

I sniffed dandelions
That grew close to me . . .
That grew by my feet
Like a big yellow sea.
I sniffed and I sniffed . . .
But what did I see?

EIGHTEEN COUSINS a-sniffing like me!

I took off my shoes
(I knew I must)
And I walked in the garden
In the soft brown dust.

I walked through grass
As high as my knee.
I walked a little faster . . .
But what did I see?

EIGHTEEN COUSINS a-walking after me!

I nibbled a carrot,
I nibbled a pea,
I nibbled a green leaf . . .
    But what did I see?

EIGHTEEN COUSINS a-nibbling like me!

I jumped on a stone,
I jumped on the grass,

I jumped on a stick
And it broke in half.

I jumped over steps
(I think there were three)

I jumped up and down . . .
But what did I see?

EIGHTEEN COUSINS a-jumping after me!

I ran down the lane,
I ran through the woods,

I ran to the meadow
As fast as I could . . .
As fast as I could
And as fast as could be.
I ran like the wind . . .
      But what did I see?

EIGHTEEN COUSINS a-running after me!

I chased a bobwhite
back to his nest,
I chased a rabbit
Stopping to rest.

I chased a butterfly,
And I chased a bee.
I chased a green 'hopper . . .
But what did I see?

EIGHTEEN COUSINS a-chasing me!

I came to a brook,
I had to stop,
But a frog splashed in
With a big ker-plop!
Up came the snails
In the little green brook,
Up came a fish
To take a good look.

Up came a beetle,
Up came a flea,
Up came a glider . . .
   But what did I see?

EIGHTEEN COUSINS a–coming close to me!

I tried to hide
But I fell on my knee,
I fell in the tall grass
And couldn't get free.

I tugged and I tugged . . .
But what did I see?

EIGHTEEN COUSINS . . . and . . . THEY CAUGHT ME!!

We laughed out loud
And we laughed out long . . .
We laughed and we laughed
Till we laughed a song.

We laughed because
>
> It's FUN to be . . .
>
> EIGHTEEN COUSINS . . . and . . .
>
> ONE LITTLE ME!!!

CAROL G. HOGAN was born in State College, Pennsylvania where she lived until graduation from Penn State College. She now makes her home in Madison, Ohio where she is the busy mother of five and the author of numerous stories for *Humpty Dumpty's Magazine* and other children's publications. *Eighteen Cousins* is Mrs. Hogan's first picture book, and the story grew out of her own happy childhood memories of visiting her "country cousins."

BEVERLY KOMODA also happened to grow up in State College, Pennsylvania, surrounded by beautiful farming countryside. She now lives in Ridgefield, New Jersey with her artist husband and their young son, Paul, who at age two, "already likes to scribble on anything he can find." Mrs. Komoda is a graduate of the Chouinard Art Institute in Los Angeles and her charming art work for children can be seen in *Douglas Saves the Day* and *The Wishing Night*.